CRAZY QUILTS

by Karen Fix Curry

GHOST LIGHT PUBLICATIONS

CRAZY QUILTS

SPECIAL NOTE

Anyone receiving permission to produce CRAZY QUILTS is required to give credit to the Author as sole and exclusive Author of the Play on the title page of all programs distributed in connection with performances of the Play and in all instances in which the title of the Play appears for purposes of advertising, publicizing or otherwise exploiting the Play and/or a production thereof. The name of the Author must appear on a separate line, in which no other name appears, immediately beneath the title and in size of type equal to 50% of the size of the largest, most prominent letter used for the title of the Play. No person, firm, or entity may receive credit larger or more prominent than that accorded the Author.

SPECIAL NOTE ON SONGS AND RECORDINGS

For performances of copyrighted songs, arrangements or recordings mentioned in these Plays, the permission of the copyright owner(s) must be obtained. Other songs, arrangements or recordings may be substituted provided permission from the copyright owner(s) of such songs, arrangements or recordings is obtained; or songs, arrangements or recordings in the public domain may be substituted.

Cover Art Design: Kerri Hellmuth
Book Design: Jonathan Cook
First Edition: March 2025
ISBN 978-1-964045-07-8

CRAZY QUILTS premiered at LAB Theater Project in Tampa, Florida on November 14, 2024. It was directed by Owen Robertson. The cast was as follows:

LISA . . . . Avry Eden
SUSAN . . . . Caroline Jett
CLARA JENKINS . . . . Judy Wilson
GARETH . . . . Rusty Gillespie
JUDY . . . . Amanda Cappello
NEWSCASTER . . . . Mike Deeson

CRAZY QUILTS

CHARACTERS

LISA
30 something, uncertain, nervous, smart.

SUSAN
60's, quiet, strong, the real leader.

CLARA JENKINS
50's, friendly, motherly.

GARETH
Late 40's, loyal, kind, helpful and gentle. A keen artistic eye.

JUDY
40's, sarcastic, vocal, determined.

NEWSCASTER
V.O. pre-recorded sound cue, may double with GARETH.

**All characters may be any ethnicity.*

PLACE

A quilt shop workroom on an island in the Puget Sound.

TIME

A few years ago.

SCENE BREAKDOWN

Scene 1 - June - making squares by hand

Scene 2 - July - Heatwave

Scene 3 - A few weeks later

Scene 4 - Late August

Scene 5 - Sept - sorting and cutting up old clothes

Scene 6 - October - at the design wall

Scene 7 - November - sewing at the machine and sorting

 *Optional Intermission

Scene 8 - The next day, hand quilting or binding a quilt edge

Scene 9 - Christmas time, a tree, snow is falling outside

Scene 10- A few weeks later, still cold out

Scene 11- Fall, two years later.

Set requirements

A door, 5 chairs, shelves, bins, and clothes, fabric, an ironing board and iron, a long table or two, a large piece of flannel over a large Styrofoam sheet used as a design wall, a coat rack and a working sewing machine.

Prop requirements

Patchwork quilts, a decorated Christmas tree with presents beneath, patchwork squares in progress, baskets with sewing notions, paper pad, and pen, purse, bins or fabric, old clothes to be cut up, a rotary cutter and mat, scissors, mugs, cake or cupcakes, a takeout bag of BBQ, crutches or medical boot.

Be imaginative. Many quilting groups throughout the country set up and tear down every time they meet, so things are portable. I encourage you to contact local quilting groups regarding quilts in progress, quilt blocks, finished quilts and such. You will learn a lot.

SCENE 1 - JUNE

Lights up on the quilting group, working on making patchwork squares by hand. The workroom is made up of folding banquet tables, chairs, a rolling set of shelves, bins of fabric, a sewing machine set up on one table with an ironing board and iron nearby.

Lisa, a 30-something enters. She is nervous and a little jumpy throughout.

LISA. *(entering)* Hello? Hello. Um. I'm looking for the quilting group. I'm Lisa. The lady in the office said I could stop in to talk to you.

CLARA. Welcome! Of course. Would you like to join us?

GARETH. Come sit over here. There's plenty of room. Have you ever quilted before?

LISA. *(sitting)* Thanks. No. I've never made anything. I was actually hoping I could interview you for the July edition of local magazine "The Cracked Crab". I've never done this, but the editor asked if I could fill in. As a favor. She said they try to highlight a different group each issue, and, well, they thought you might be a good feature next month.

(The ladies react excitedly.)

CLARA. Aren't you sweet? And they thought of us? Why we're just a simple little quilting group. I don't see why anyone would be interested.

JUDY. Speak for yourself, Clara. I think it's about time. I'm Judy. And this is Gareth. And she's Clara. She fancies herself the leader of our little group, but that's not so, is it Clara?

GARETH. That's enough, Judy. You're just sore because you're the junior member. We've been together for a long time. We don't always get along, but we all like making quilts, so... *(shrugs)* What is it you'd like to know?

(Lisa gets a pen and pad of paper out of her purse.)

LISA. Let me get something to take some notes. I've never done this before, so I'm sorry in advance if I kind of wander all over. They gave me a few questions to help me get started. Here it is. *(reading)* How did you all get together? And how long have you been a group? And how many are in the group?

CLARA. There's four of us. There should be five, but then Charlene… well, that doesn't concern you, now does it? I'm Clara.

(Lisa takes notes throughout.)

JUDY. She knows.

GARETH. I'm Gareth. What else did you want to know?

LISA. How long have you been a group?

GARETH. The group's been around forever.

CLARA. Some of us joined later. Like Gareth, and Judy here. And there's Susan.

LISA. Uh-huh.

CLARA. She's the oldest member.

LISA. Really?

GARETH. She's been here the longest. You could say she started the whole thing.

LISA. Oh? So you started the group? How did you do that, Susan?

JUDY. She won't tell you. She's kind of quiet, aren't you Susan? It's high time everyone knew, if you ask me.

GARETH. No one's asking you. Remember Judy, you're the junior member.

CLARA. We've been together 32 years all together. That would be Susan, and me, and of course, poor Charlene.

JUDY. Some of us live here in town but Gareth and I both take the ferry. What about you?

LISA. That's where I've seen you, on the ferry. *(beat)* So, what do you do with all the quilts you make?

CLARA. We donate them. They go to local women's shelters mostly, but we've raffled off some to raise funds to pay for supplies like batting and such. Would you like to see one?

LISA. That would be great. I can take a picture for the Cracked Crab.

(Gareth and Judy pick up a folded quilt and hold it up, standing far away from the quilt in order to avoid being in the photo.)

Wow. It's beautiful!

GARETH. Get a close up.

JUDY. Yeah, I'm a mess today.

(Lisa moves closer to the quilt. She snaps a photo. They fold up the quilt.)

LISA. I wish I could make something like that. Where do you get all the fabric?

CLARA. It's donated clothes. And from our fabric stash. We almost never have to buy fabric, unless we want a large piece for the back.

(Lisa takes notes again.)

LISA. Do you think I need to mention your names? I don't

really know how much info I need to make the article long enough.

CLARA. I think it'll be fine if you just write about the group.

LISA. Are you sure?

(Everyone immediately agrees a little too much.)

Well, OK. Does your group have a name?

JUDY. Crazy Quilts. Just call us the Crazy Quilts group.

GARETH. Crazy Quilts are a kind of quilt pattern. They're made up of fabric scraps, you see? And we use a lot of scraps.

LISA. Oh, I get it.

(Lisa writes another note and closes her notebook, rises, and starts to leave.)

Well thanks for letting me interview you. I've never done this before, but I think with the photo and all, I should be able to write 100 words and fill a page. It makes me wish I knew how to quilt. You've all been really nice to me. I don't have many, you know, friends.

CLARA. You're welcome to come back again. We'd love to have you join us.

LISA. I'm pretty busy. I'll have to think it over.

JUDY. We meet again in two weeks. 10:00am. Please come.

GARETH. You could start off with something easy like ironing or sorting.

(Judy glares at Gareth.)

JUDY. Or something fun like picking a pattern.

LISA. *(hedging)* I don't know. I'll think about it. Thanks, everybody. This was nice. Really nice. I've just got a lot on my plate now. Maybe another time.

CLARA. Think about it.

GARETH. We'd all love to see you again.

LISA. I'm awfully busy -

JUDY. Remember. Two weeks from today.

LISA. At 10:00. Got it. Bye.

    (Lisa flees the room.)

CLARA. So? What do you think?

SUSAN. Clara, I think you were right about her.

GARETH. She was nervous as a cat. Poor darling.

JUDY. She seems nice. I feel sorry for her.

SUSAN. Now we wait and see if she comes back.

    Lights down.

SCENE 2 - JULY

Lights up. The quilters are busy sewing. Judy rises and crosses to open the door. She pumps the door open and closed in an effort to cool off.

JUDY. There's no breeze. It's so hot! I'm cooking.

GARETH. How can 85 feel so hot?

CLARA. It's the humidity. The joys of living in the Pacific Northwest.

GARETH. Well it feels like 95 to me. Do we still have that fan in the back?

(Gareth exits.)

CLARA. Has anyone seen Lisa in town or anything? I was really hoping she'd come back.

(Gareth enters with a free-standing fan, plugs it in and turns it on.)

SUSAN. Oh thank you, God. It works.

JUDY. No. And it's been a month.

GARETH. It takes time. You remember how it was.

JUDY. She chickened out.

CLARA. Well, I'm not giving up yet. This is only the second meeting since we met her.

GARETH. She seemed genuinely interested at one point.

JUDY. Until you wanted to give her ironing. I'd be running for the hills if all I was going to get to do was iron!

GARETH. I was trying to think of something easy.

JUDY. Right. Let's all join the quilting group so we can iron. My life's dream.

GARETH. Point taken.

CLARA. We can't get too excited yet. Remember, Gareth, how long it took you to come back.

GARETH. Barb thought I was trying to hook up with someone. The first time I came, she followed me and I had to go to the hardware store instead. And the second. And the third.

CLARA. But you made it.

GARETH. Only when I told her I volunteered to install a set of shelves for the center. She laughed at me. Told me they'd have to tear it out and rebuild it.

JUDY. Oh Gareth! That's just cruel.

GARETH. Verbal abuse was her go to. I still replay her cuts in my dreams.

CLARA. Did the therapist have anything to help you with that?

GARETH. You mean drugs? Yeah, in the beginning. I'm trying to use coping strategies, but I still have flashbacks.

CLARA. Medication is a good alternative in a pinch.

GARETH. Just don't get dependent on them. I know.

CLARA. Did you all see the paper this morning?

GARETH. I haven't read it yet.

SUSAN. So sad. It breaks my heart.

GARETH. What happened?

CLARA. You remember a few years ago, we reached out to Jeannie, that sweet lady with the teenage boys?

JUDY. Who?

CLARA. She was before your time.

GARETH. Of course. What a horrible situation. I wish she'd taken us up on our offer.

CLARA. She was just too frightened. It's harder when you have children to think about.

SUSAN. I admire that she said she'd keep our secret.

GARETH. I always hoped she'd change her mind. What about her?

CLARA. She was murdered yesterday. The paper said it was intruders.

GARETH. I don't believe it. Not for a minute.

JUDY. Poor Jeannie.

SUSAN. We can't save everyone.

CLARA. The youngest son just went off to college last fall.

GARETH. What a tragedy.

JUDY. Oh my God! It's Lisa! She's here! Everybody. Act natural.

(Judy rushes to take a seat. Lisa enters, hesitantly.)

LISA. Hello? Oh. Uh hi everybody.

CLARA. Hello! Look Susan, Lisa's here.

LISA. I'm not staying. I just dropped by to give you a copy of the Cracked Crab. In case you didn't pick one up. Anyway...

(Lisa hands a small freebie magazine to Gareth.)

GARETH. Were your ears burning? We were just talking about you.

CLARA. And what a nice time we had meeting you.

LISA. I'm sorry I didn't come to the last meeting. *(beat)* I wanted to make sure you got a copy.

CLARA. No need for excuses dear. We're glad you're here.

LISA. I have to get back. I have some things I need to get done at home, and Mark's expecting me -

GARETH. Come sit over here. Would you like some iced tea?

(Gareth rises and pours some iced tea for Lisa.)

LISA. That sounds wonderful! It's crazy hot out there.

JUDY. Hottest it's been in almost a hundred years. I heard it on the morning news.

(Gareth hands her the iced tea.)

LISA. Thanks.

GARETH. It has lemon in it. I hope that's all right.

LISA. Sounds perfect. Look, I can't stay long. I really do need to get back. I was wondering... well I thought that... is it too late to uh... give your group a try? Maybe in a few weeks? If I can manage it.

(All reassure her.)

CLARA. We're glad you decided to come. Maybe we can start by telling you a little more about it. What we do, just some details.

JUDY. We're always willing to add new members, if they qualify.

GARETH. We have some pretty specific guidelines. Most people who come just end up visiting and don't stay with the group.

CLARA. We have to be very careful who we accept.

LISA. Because of their sewing ability, right? I can't sew a stitch.

GARETH. No! Anyone can learn to sew. That's the least important part.

LISA. Then what are you looking for in a member?

JUDY. They have to have a shared background.

GARETH. Not culturally or ethnically, obviously. A shared past.

CLARA. A common life experience.

LISA. Like you're all widows or single parents? Like that?

CLARA. Something like that.

(They all exchange looks.)

And if they do, they are in.

LISA. So what qualifies one to join?

GARETH. It's not exactly one specific thing. Right Susan?

(Susan smiles and nods.)

CLARA. Why don't you tell us a little bit about yourself. I think we can show you how we decide.

LISA. Oh. OK. What do you want to know?

GARETH. Did you grow up around here?

LISA. Oh yes. I've lived my entire life right here on the Puget Sound. I've always been an island girl.

JUDY. That's in your favor. Pretty rural?

LISA. Yes. We actually lived on a small island when I was growing up that you couldn't even get to by ferry. Dad had to take us back and forth by boat.

(They smile and nod.)

CLARA. Not much in the way of social services, right? No fire department. No police.

LISA. Yeah. It was OK though, because the residents pretty much knew each other, and kept tabs on what was going on. We had a neighbor who got drunk every Friday night, like clockwork. And when he got a little too buzzed, some of the men would head over and make sure he made it home, stuff like that.

GARETH. That must've been a very tight knit community.

LISA. It was. I live on Guemas Island now. At least it has a ferry, and we can come to the mainland. But it still has that small town thing. It's like everyone knows everybody else's business, but still there are a lot of secrets.

JUDY. Are there ever.

CLARA. You know, sometimes, bad things happen on little islands.

GARETH. And people disappear.

JUDY. For good reasons. Some very good reasons.

CLARA. And there's nothing like a group of friends, really close friends, who understand, and help out when bad times come.

JUDY. And listen when you need to talk about it.

GARETH. And help solve problems you may be having.

LISA. Sometimes I feel like there's no one to talk to.

GARETH. Like personal stuff.

JUDY. Bad stuff.

CLARA. Like Charlene. Huh, Susan?

SUSAN. Sometimes you just gotta have a friend when times get to be more than you can bear. Charlene was there for me. I'll never forget that.

LISA. What happened?

(They pause their sewing. They exchange looks. Susan nods.)

SUSAN. You can't tell anyone about this. Nobody can know about this.

(Lisa sets down her iced tea, nodding. She's nervous.)

I was twenty-two. It was the 70's and I met this guy Greg. I thought he was so nice and kind, and loving, and he was, the whole time we dated. He brought me flowers. He surprised me with little presents. He even carved me a ring out of a whale tooth he found on the beach. Scrimshawed all over that ring. It was amazing. So, even though my parents thought it was a bad idea, I ran off with him and got married just three months later. That's when the beatings started. Just little stuff at first. He'd get mad about something and give me a little whack. The laundry wasn't done, or dinner was late, I didn't laugh at his jokes. It stung, but it didn't leave any mark, and after he was so sorry.

JUDY. They're always so sorry after.

(All nod. Lisa joins in.)

SUSAN. You ever have something like that happen to you?

LISA. No! Not like that.

CLARA. We've all been there.

GARETH. That's another point in your favor of joining, hon.

SUSAN. Next thing you know, he's shoving me up against the wall, and throwing me across the room, and I can't go out 'cause I'm covered in bruises. And I didn't know what else to do. So I called Charlene.

GARETH. God bless her.

LISA. She helped you get out?

SUSAN. It's an island. I'm on this little island. There's no getting out. Who's gonna take my word for it, but someone who lived through it too? Certainly not any of Greg's friends and family. But Charlene figured out a way to help.

(Susan stops, unsure whether to continue.)

GARETH. We heard about what you've been going through,

LISA. We wanted to help you out.

LISA. What? What do you mean?

JUDY. Little islands have big ears, hon. And we heard what Mark has been up to. What you've had to deal with.

LISA. Wait. What have you heard about Mark? He loves me.

(Clara takes Lisa's hand.)

CLARA. And we want to help you. The way Charlene helped SUSAN. Only we've improved on it over the years. You see, Susan helped me.

(Clara squeezes Susan's hand.)

GARETH. And Clara helped me.

(Gareth reaches and holds Clara's hand.)

JUDY. And Gareth helped me.

(Judy pats Gareth's knee.)

And now I want to help you. We all want to.

CLARA. I know why you think you came here, but we set this up. The interview, everything.

LISA. I don't understand.

JUDY. We're going to help you. With Mark.

LISA. You're what?

(Lisa bolts up from her seat. She paces and checks the entrance door to make sure Mark isn't within earshot as she speaks.)

Are you out of your mind? No no no no no. I don't need that kind of help. I'm fine. We're fine.

SUSAN. You don't act fine, dear.

LISA. I don't know what you're talking about. Who said? Who said I need help? I'm fine.

SUSAN. We have our ways, and we know you are definitely not fine. Honey, you are so isolated.

GARETH. You have no neighbors within a mile of you.

CLARA. And no one ever comes to visit.

JUDY. You have horrible cellphone reception. You can't even call for help.

LISA. Have you been spying-

SUSAN. -You're trapped.

CLARA. You need allies.

GARETH. People who know what it is to feel alone and powerless.

JUDY. With no way out.

SUSAN. Who want to help you. You can't do this by yourself. You need friends.

LISA. I can't. I can't! You're wrong. I don't know who told you but I'm fine. I'm happy. It's not like that.

(Lisa grabs her things and crosses to leave.)

I'm sure you mean well, but I don't need your help! I have to go.

(Lisa exits.)

JUDY. Well that went well.

CLARA. Now we wait.

SUSAN. And hope she comes back. God willing.

GARETH. Well I hope she doesn't report us to the police.

Lights down.

SCENE 3 – A FEW WEEKS LATER

The group busy working on quilts. Music plays. Lisa bursts in. She is in long sleeves.

LISA. I need to get out of here. I need to go far away, someplace safe. Someplace he can't find me. I tried to leave him, but he found out. Oh God help me how do I get out? -- I need help. Please. You have to help me. I thought he was going to... Please. You have to help me!

(They all stand and rush to her. Susan takes her in her arms, as they gather around. Lisa winces from the hugs.)

SUSAN. Thank God. You're safe.

CLARA. What has he done to you? Oh Lisa.

LISA. It's nothing.

GARETH. It's not nothing.

CLARA. Here. Careful.

(Clara starts to help her remove her sweater, revealing bruises. Lisa quickly covers them back up.)

JUDY. That asshole. *(*Optional - That scumbag.)*

LISA. I'm sorry I didn't want to listen before. I couldn't admit it. Even to myself.

SUSAN. We've all been there. We understand. Clara, get some ice please.

(Clara exits.)

GARETH. It took me forever to get up the guts to come. Good for you.

LISA. I didn't know where else to go.

JUDY. I kept trying to leave. But he always found out where I was and brought me back. It's not like Sleeping with the Enemy. He always figured it out.

SUSAN. Now you just come sit down over here and let's have a nice chat and explain how it works.

(Clara enters with a towel of ice and gives it to Lisa.)

LISA. Thank you. I just kept thinking about what you said. How everyone needs friends who understand.

GARETH. You did the right thing, Lisa.

LISA. How did you know... about me and... everything?

SUSAN. You'll laugh. Who's the one person who sees you almost every day?

LISA. I don't know. Nobody.

CLARA. Lisa, I work at the post office. And I have a lot of friends there. Co-workers.

LISA. I don't understand.

CLARA. Lisa, we gossip. Who we saw, what we heard. Crazy things we see and hear while out delivering the mail. Like screaming.

GARETH. She takes notes and we follow up.

CLARA. For them it's just a juicy tidbit at work.

SUSAN. Clara brings us the names and addresses.

JUDY. We've been watching you for over a year.

LISA. A year? What if he finds out? Oh my God. Do you know what he's going to do to me if he finds out?

SUSAN. He hasn't, has he?

LISA. But why me?

SUSAN. Because you have no one else. You seemed so hopeless.

CLARA. We've all been there. Blaming yourself, buying

into the lie that you are the reason he acts the way he does. But Lisa. You deserve better.

JUDY. We want you to be able to have a future, and take control like we have, and make your own decisions, and sleep well at night, and all the things we know you have hidden away right now.

GARETH. *(rising)* We've all helped each other and no one has ever found out.

CLARA. And by helping each other, they can never pin it on the abused spouse. It's a wonderful plan.

SUSAN. Charlene thought it up. Only she didn't quite figure out every angle, and God how I miss her.

GARETH. She just didn't account for everything.

CLARA. But we've figured it out now, and it's worked perfectly since then.

SUSAN. Spouses die every day.

(Silence as Lisa looks at the group, shocked, but then understanding.)

GARETH. They fall off ladders.

JUDY. They drown.

CLARA. They drive into trees.

SUSAN. They go hunting and never return.

JUDY. And the only thing you have to do is join the quilting group. You'll be here when it happens. Making these lovely patchwork quilts.

LISA. You mean you…

CLARA. That was my idea.

GARETH. You always were good at recycling.

JUDY. Nothing gets wasted. Except him. And look what lovely things we do with his clothes after! That's the best things they ever do. Provide fabric for quilts.

(Lisa rises, uncertain. Judy also rises and takes Lisa in her arms. She carefully gives her a motherly hug. Everyone gathers around and joins in the hug. Susan hands Lisa a quilt block to stitch.)

SUSAN. Here. Let me show you how to do it.

Lights down.

SCENE 4 – AUGUST

Judy, and Gareth are seated. Lisa enters.

GARETH. Look at the early bird.

LISA. Sorry I don't have much time today. Mark said I had to be done by the time he's finished at the hardware store. I figure I've got 45 minutes tops.

JUDY. Everything OK?

LISA. He's gotten a lot harder to deal with since I joined. I'm getting a lot of flack about how much I'm gone.

GARETH. It's twice a month.

LISA. He was bad, but never like this. He made me choose between this and my morning walk. He says I'm meeting up with somebody. Like Gareth.

GARETH. Me?

LISA. He saw you through the window and now he thinks I'm cheating on him with you.

GARETH. Oh, honey!

LISA. The truth is... well, I almost didn't join because of you.

JUDY. Because men make you nervous.

(Lisa nods.)

LISA. And then you were so nice, and I realized you were a victim too and -

GARETH. Thank you. That means a lot.

LISA. Anyway, Mark is pressuring me to quit.

GARETH. So you give up your walk.

JUDY. He's a real piece of work.

LISA. It's not just my walk today. It's all my morning walks. So now I have no time when I'm alone unless Mark takes off somewhere.

GARETH. What about when he goes to work?

LISA. He works out of the garage so he's home all day unless he needs something.

GARETH. Sorry. I forgot.

JUDY. He makes yard art, right?

LISA. Carved logs, you know, with a chainsaw. Bears, eagles, fake totem poles. Stuff like that. Most of it is sold to tourists.

JUDY. Nothing says the Pacific Northwest like a chain-sawed bear.

GARETH. Not exactly a safe environment either, I bet. Chainsaws. *(shudders)*

LISA. *(shaking her head)* Or a clean house. He leaves sawdust like a trail.

GARETH. Well at least you got away for a little while today.

LISA. And I need to borrow something to take home to work on. He's already asking where this quilt I'm making is.

JUDY. Oh yeah, like you can whip out a complete quilt in three meetings.

GARETH. JUDY. Look, I'm sure we have a completed top in the bin you can take with you. It'll make you look like you're doing a lot.

JUDY. I'll get it.

(Judy crosses to get it.)

GARETH. All it needs is to have stray threads trimmed, pick the loose threads off the top side, and make sure it gets a nice pressing so it will be ready to go to the long arm quilter.

LISA. The long arm?

GARETH. That's Clara. She takes them home and puts them on her big quilting machine and does all the quilting. You know, those fancy stitches all over. And when they come back, we trim the edges and sew on the binding and label.

(Judy enters with a large bag.)

JUDY. Here you go. It'll make you look like you're really productive. It's a queen size. And I put a couple of Clara's zucchinis in the bottom of the bag. She's drowning in them.

LISA. Thanks.

GARETH. Hang onto the top as long as you like. You can swap it for one that just needs binding later.

LISA. This should help fend him off. At least for a while.

GARETH. Have you given any more thought to what you might do, you know, after, for a job?

LISA. I don't know. It's strange to think about it.

GARETH. Well let me know. I can reach out to some people I know -

JUDY. He got me my start in property appraisal. I had zero job experience, so I jumped at it. You get to make your own hours and it's a great way to snoop around and find stuff out about people.

LISA. I'll keep it in mind. Actually, I've always been more of a writer. Maybe journalism, radio, tv documentaries?

JUDY. Not many jobs like that around here.

GARETH. I'm sure we can help you find something that interests you.

LISA. Where's Susan and Clara today?

JUDY. Susan is at the nursery school. She lets them play with her old stethoscope, and takes their temps, puts on pretend bandages and stuff. She's a retired nurse.

LISA. That's so sweet.

GARETH. They usually call her to come over when they're shorthanded. She loves playing with the little ones, and they love their "Grandma Susie".

JUDY. And Clara is working on her long arm today. She's got AC at home. This building is ten degrees cooler than my place. So...

(Judy shrugs. Sound of a car horn.)

LISA. That's him. He couldn't have gone clear to the hardware store and back already.

GARETH. He's testing you. Barbara used to do that. She'd show up unexpectedly and be in a horrible mood when she found out I was where I said I was. I think she was disappointed that she didn't catch me.

JUDY. Shaun was the worst. Showed up early or left me waiting until everything was closed and it was dark and freezing out. *(sighs)* Well you better get going before his majesty decides to take it out on you.

LISA. Right. Thanks for this.

(Lisa exits.)

JUDY. I saw that big pickup drive by at least twice before he honked. I hate how predictable they are.

GARETH. I just hope he doesn't make her pay for stopping in.

JUDY. Amen to that.

Lights down.

SCENE 5 – SEPTEMBER

Everyone is working on sorting through clothes in some boxes. Lisa has settled in, standing at a cutting table with a cutting wheel and ruler. She pulls a shirt from a box.

JUDY. Did anyone watch the Harvest Parade? This is the first year I've missed it.

LISA. I've never been. Mark says it's stupid and a waste of time so…

(Everyone murmurs understanding.)

SUSAN. I go every year.

CLARA. You're in charge every year, Susan.

JUDY. Was there anything new? I completely overslept. I love the parade!

SUSAN. We added 4-H animals this year. Goats, llamas, cows.

CLARA. And a pig!

JUDY. Great. I missed the llamas.

GARETH. And one goat ate a little girl's doll.

CLARA. Was that what that horrible shrieking was about? Poor baby.

SUSAN. The parade committee has promised her a replacement.

GARETH. You mean you promised to replace it.

JUDY. Better pray it's not an American Girl doll. Do you know how much those things cost?

GARETH. Ooo. This will be fabulous for the quilt! Feel this.

It's luscious.

CLARA. I found another one.

SUSAN. Put them on the table. And then we need to discuss what pattern we want to do.

(Gareth takes his find and crosses to Clara and gets hers, then takes them to Lisa at the cutting table.)

LISA. This is a really nice shirt. You really want me to cut it up?

JUDY. *(rising)* Slice away, hon. Check out the lipstick on the collar. Classic.

LISA. Oh my God.

(Lisa slices the shirt sleeves off with a cutting wheel. Cutting the clothing continues throughout.)

CLARA. You should see what she does with the trouser crotches.

JUDY. Hey, I save the legs for stuff.

CLARA. She takes them home and burns them.

SUSAN. Unless she hacks them to bits with the rotary cutter.

JUDY. I'm making sure no part of anything his cheating dick has touched ever touches anyone ever again.

GARETH. She finds it very cathartic.

CLARA. Do we have to cut this up? Look at this.

GARETH. That fabric is too fabulous to be given to Goodwill.

JUDY. There's too much history in that one. He wore that on our honeymoon. Cut it up.

SUSAN. Lisa? You were telling us about Mark.

LISA. Right. Um. Let's see. *(beat)* He drinks. But not like he's an alcoholic or anything. Um. He likes to speed when he drives. And he doesn't wear a seatbelt. And he turned off all the car alerts. You know, the buzzers?

SUSAN. We've done a car wreck. Best to not repeat previous endeavors.

GARETH. So that lets out falls, drowning, and hunting accidents.

CLARA. Unless it's a different kind of fall or whatever.

SUSAN. True.

LISA. He's into sports. Like skiing? He's really good at that.

(Susan writes.)

He takes tons of vitamins. Poison maybe?

SUSAN. An autopsy would figure that right out. We don't want them coming after you. But thanks for thinking of it.

JUDY. Maybe he could do it. You said earlier he's a little into kink, right?

SUSAN. Judy, we are not going to hang him and call it auto erotic asphyxiation!

JUDY. Fine.

GARETH. Even if they did find Jeffrey Epstein that way.

JUDY. Fine. Fine! I still think it's something we should put on the list.

CLARA. Susan, go ahead a write it down. We can always reconsider if we don't come up with a better idea.

SUSAN. I suppose you're right.

(Susan writes.)

CLARA. Can you think of anything else that might work, Lisa? Hobbies, interests, anything at all that might give us an opening.

JUDY. Chainsaw accident!

EVERYONE. No!

JUDY. Killjoys.

LISA. He's always wanted to learn how to fly a plane.

GARETH. So what? Are we all going to have to pony up for flying lessons and sabotage a plane just so he can die in a plane crash?

JUDY. Gareth's right. Flying lessons cost thousands of dollars. That's not going to happen.

(Susan holds up a hand for silence.)

SUSAN. LISA. What about... a parachute jump?

LISA. How am I going to get him to do that? He's never talked about wanting to before.

GARETH. You'd have to sabotage a folded parachute.

JUDY. Two parachutes. They wear a backup in case the first one doesn't deploy.

CLARA. How do you know that?

JUDY. Because, Clara, I spent my summers in college working at a skydiving center. My nickname was Geronimo.

GARETH. Is it even possible?

SUSAN. What do you suggest? This is your area after all.

JUDY. If I worked there, I'd just trash talk him into it.

GARETH. Nothing pushes a narcissist's buttons like being told he can't do something.

SUSAN. Well Judy?

JUDY. It might work. But there's a ton of things that can go wrong.

GARETH. How do we get him to do it?

JUDY. Maybe he could win a gift certificate.

CLARA. Maybe.

SUSAN. Lisa, what do you think?

LISA. He might.

SUSAN. OK. So by the time we get together again, let's all do some more research and see if we can come up with some details, OK?

JUDY. And I'll go get get my old job back at the skydiving center.

GARETH. Sounds good.

CLARA. *(aside to Judy)* Do you think it will work?

JUDY. It better.

Lights down.

SCENE 6 – OCTOBER

The quilting group is standing and discussing the design wall, rearranging blocks of patchwork in a pattern.

CLARA. *(moving squares)* I think those should go there and these should go here.

GARETH. But that completely destroys the effect. What about this? *(arranging squares)*

SUSAN. You have such a good eye, Gareth.

LISA. I like that.

(Judy enters, rushing and pulling off her heavy coat.)

JUDY. Well, so much for the parachute idea.

(All react.)

Ah, heat! It is ridiculously cold out there. I'm freezing.

CLARA. Where have you been? You're late. Again.

SUSAN. I brought hot chocolate today. Would you like some?

JUDY. That sounds wonderful.

(Susan gets up to get a mug.)

I just went to the Skydive place on the mainland, and they don't do solo jumps. Ever. Unless you've had like a million lessons.

(Takes mug.)

Thanks.

SUSAN. Oh no.

GARETH. And I thought it was such an inspired idea.

JUDY. And to top it off, they wouldn't hire me anyway. Now they only hire certified instructors! I worked for them for four years! *(takes sip)* Ooo, this is really good.

SUSAN. It's the Bailey's.

CLARA. We'll just have to think of something else.

JUDY. I was really looking forward to working there again.

LISA. Now what'll we do?

SUSAN. I'm sure we can come up with something.

JUDY. And in the meantime, Lisa will just keep being his personal punching bag.

(All stop and look at LISA.)

LISA. I asked you not to say anything!

(All react ad lib OMG, are you OK, etc. Lisa clutches herself trying to hide her arms and neck. She attempts to leave. Clara stops her. She puts her arm around her.)

CLARA. There are no secrets between us here, LISA.

(Lisa and Clara cross back to the group.)

SUSAN. We have to think of something. Fast.

JUDY. He's getting worse, isn't he?

LISA. It's not that bad.

JUDY. Oh yes it is. I saw you putting groceries in the car the other day and you could barely lift the bags. They need to know.

LISA. He's never done anything this bad before. It was my fault.

CLARA. Don't say that. Don't you ever take the blame for his horrible behavior, hon.

LISA. I can't help it. I forgot to buy extra beer. *(beat)* All day every day it's nothing but what a worthless waste of humanity I am. *(imitating him)* I'm lucky to have him. What a terrible job I do. Nobody could possibly ever want me.

CLARA. That's terrible!

JUDY. Classic dickhead bullshit* *(Optional - misogynist crap).* Like it's your fault for not living up to his impossible expectations.

LISA. *(imitating him)* You're clumsy and you can't do anything right. You're lucky I take care of you. You need to straighten up. You know how I get when you make me mad!

GARETH. And afterword he's so sorry.

CLARA. And then he buys you something like flowers -

GARETH. Or a new watch -

JUDY. Or a fancy dinner out - I was so terrified when we were going out to a fancy dinner. He expected me to get all dressed up -

CLARA. And you had to figure out how to hide all the bruises.

(Judy nods.)

LISA. I've been being told it's my fault for years now. *(imitating)* "No one else cares about you but me".

GARETH. *(talking over her)* You're among friends, Lisa. We all care about you.

LISA. - and don't even think about anybody else because then I'm a whore if a man looks at me and a bitch if I have an opinion of my own. No matter what I do I can't get anything right, and it's so hard to not make him mad when he says I screw up all the time.

JUDY. Even if you did everything perfectly, he'd find a reason to get mad at you. I know.

GARETH. You're safe here.

SUSAN. And we all want you safe. For good.

LISA. I know. I'm grateful, really. But then he shows up to pick me up. I just see the truck coming down the road and I'm shaking. I tried to talk to his Mom about it the first time it happened and she said "My son isn't like that. You just need to try a little harder."

JUDY. She's the last one you should talk to. She was probably abused by his dad.

LISA. Yeah, I know. She told me some real horror stories after he died. *(imitating her)* But Mark would never do that.

CLARA. We should get Judy on track pronto.

LISA. On track?

GARETH. Talk to her in public. Run into her when you're out with Mark. Get her familiar to Mark.

CLARA. They don't have to be friends, he just needs to know she's no threat. Just text her whenever you two are going out somewhere, and she'll make a point of being there. Simple.

LISA. But I never have friends over. I'm not even allowed to have my mom over. I always have to come up with some lame reason why she can't come.

GARETH. She doesn't have to come to your house. Just run into her when you're out.

JUDY. And if he goes someplace without you, I can be there too.

LISA. Like when he goes to breakfast at the diner every Saturday with his old school buddies?

JUDY. I'm adding that to my calendar right now.

(Judy gets her phone and types.)

SUSAN. Whatever we do come up with, it will give Judy an

edge by being a familiar face. Like Charlene was.

GARETH. And when it is time to, you know, he won't think twice about Judy offering to help hold the ladder or whatever, you see?

LISA. You never told me what happened, Susan. To Charlene.

CLARA. Oh Lisa…

SUSAN. It's why we are so careful, Lisa. Charlene learned a hard lesson and we've all never forgotten. *(beat)* Greg, my late husband, was an avid hunter. We had trophies all over the house, antlers hanging over the workshop, you know the type. And the tougher the hunt, the better he liked it. Now Charlene knew he loved a good challenge, and she hunted with her dad when she was growing up.

CLARA. Susan used to call her Annie Oakley, because she was such a good shot.

SUSAN. She did target competitions, and even considered trying out for the Olympics at one point.

CLARA. Greg was really intimidated. He hated that he could be outshot by a woman.

SUSAN. So one day Charlene came by to pick me up to go shopping.

CLARA. Greg refused to buy her a car.

JUDY. Are you going to tell this story? Go on, Susan.

SUSAN. So Greg was there when I got picked up. I usually tried to go when he wasn't home because, well, you know.

LISA. Yeah. I totally get it.

SUSAN. I thought when he confronted Charlene that she'd just leave, but suddenly there they are, talking guns and hunts and all, and a few weeks later Greg up and invites her along on his bighorn sheep hunt.

CLARA. That's a really big deal. There are only a few permits for that hunt each year.

SUSAN. Greg just wanted her along to show off how great a hunter he was. He knew it was really a rigorous trek up the mountain, and you have to be a crack shot to get one, then you have to get it down the mountain and back to your camp.

LISA. It sounds horrible.

SUSAN. Well Charlene always loved a challenge. So she encouraged him.

LISA. And made him think she was a friend.

GARETH. Or at least not a threat.

SUSAN. Charlene and I talked about it later. She knew that there wouldn't be anyone else around and well, her dad had abused her mom for years.

LISA. She killed her father?!

SUSAN. No! No. He died in a hunting accident. Charlene knew how much better their lives were once he was gone, and she vowed to never let someone she loved go through that again. So she went hunting with Greg.

LISA. What happened?

GARETH. This is the worst part.

SUSAN. I don't know. Neither of them ever returned, and their bodies were never found.

CLARA. They did find Greg's truck still parked a couple of weeks later.

SUSAN. It took years until they were both finally declared dead. The weather was bad, and there was an early snowstorm. Maybe they got caught in it and froze.

Maybe she shot him, and he killed her. I don't know. I like to think that she got the better of him, and then she got lost trying to get back to the truck in the storm.

LISA. That's terrible.

SUSAN. So now we plan them out. Every detail. I knew she was going to kill him. I've spent years... I miss her. You know there are still times I feel guilty that I don't miss him, but I don't. She saved me. God bless Charlene. She said she was going to protect me from him, and she did.

LISA. I'm so lucky to have found you.

SUSAN. And we're glad we found you in time.

Lights down.

SCENE 7 – NOVEMBER

Gareth, and Clara enter, pulling a rolling shelf stacked with plastic bins of fabric. There's a coat rack of coats, an ironing board and iron, and a long table with a sewing machine at one end, where Susan sits sewing a quilt top. A couple of bins are brought to the table as the quilters chat.

GARETH. How's your back, Clara?

CLARA. It's doing better. Thanks for the back rub.

GARETH. Anything for my favorite mail carrier. Is it really busy already?

CLARA. More like slammed. All those online orders and catalogs. Ho ho ho.

GARETH. *(digging in a bin)* Whose clothes are these? Hm. At least this guy had great taste. I just wish they favored bolder colors.

SUSAN. We always manage. Clara, why don't you cut those up?

(Clara holds up a nice item of clothing.)

CLARA. Fancy.

GARETH. Those were Barb's. Oh wow. I'd forgotten about that. Barb never looked good in it, but she sure thought she did. She spent a small fortune on clothes. I'm glad they are finally good for something.

CLARA. Look at this designer label.

SUSAN. Where's Judy?

GARETH. Maybe off to visit her folks for Thanksgiving.

SUSAN. I don't know about you, but I don't miss all that cooking. Now I just show up at my neighbor's with a box of chocolates, and a centerpiece. It's one day and done.

CLARA. She told me she was staying on the island this year. She's late. As usual. I think she does it to avoid having to set up.

SUSAN. Now Clara…

CLARA. Last here. First to leave. Just saying…

GARETH. These are cut.

CLARA. Just put them in the bins over there. You weren't here last week. We sorted all the fabric by color last time. Check it out. And... I brought pumpkin pie for later.

GARETH. It's a good thing we only meet every two weeks.

(He pats his stomach and begins putting fabric in the bin on the shelf. He pulls out a square. It sets him off and drops it, shaking.)

Oh my God. I just had a moment. How can it be so many years later and I still... it still doesn't feel like she's gone.

SUSAN. It takes time but you get there.

GARETH. It's been what? Eight years? No, twelve. I still turn around and expect to see her. You know? Sometimes at night, when the house is really still, I think I can hear her downstairs, and I'm terrified. And I have to remind myself she's gone.

CLARA. Oh Gareth. I'm sorry

GARETH. I still hear her voice sometimes, in my dreams. Like, "Hear that? That's the sound of nobody caring what you think." and "Your mother should have thrown you away, you're such a disappointment."

CLARA. You are the kindest, gentlest man I've ever known. You didn't deserve any of that.

GARETH. I know. We've all been through it. Sometimes though, the flashbacks seem to ramp up. She made me feel like all the badness was my fault.

CLARA. It'll get better. You'll see. One day you'll just realize you're OK. It's been months since the last time, remember? You're doing better. Really. Look, I'll take this bin home and cut them later.

(Clara closes the bin and sets it aside. She gets something from Gareth's bin to cut.)

GARETH. Thanks, Clara.

(Enter Judy in a rush, nervous, with a venti coffee.)

JUDY. Sorry sorry! So sorry!

(Judy peels off jacket, scarf, gloves and hat. Everyone greets her.)

I lost track of the time! The storm knocked out the power this morning, and I was headed over and I thought I had time to drive through Shipwreck Coffee and grab a latte, and then I saw Shaun's truck go by and I just... I know it's been sold for years, and Shaun doesn't drive it anymore but I guess... anyway. I'm here.

CLARA. You too? What is it about this weather?

JUDY. I know! It's just that I saw the truck and bam! I'm hearing him all over again harping on about how we don't need two cars, and if I didn't squander my allowance maybe we'd have money for things 'cause it's my fault we're so strapped and I just... lost it.

GARETH. Come here. We both need a hug.

(Gareth hugs Judy while Clara rises and looks out the window downstage)

SUSAN. I think it's because we're stuck inside. Kind of cabin fever.

CLARA. It's snowing in the mountains.

SUSAN. Take a deep breath.

(Judy takes a breath.)

There you go.

JUDY. *(shudders)* I should have sold that truck to a dealer. I feel like I see it two or three times a week and still -

CLARA. You're just nervous, hon. We've all had our moments.

JUDY. Susan doesn't. You're always so calm.

CLARA. She used to. Me too.

(Clara crosses to SUSAN.)

SUSAN. You learn to cope. And heal. We all went through it.

GARETH. You're doing fine.

JUDY. Has anyone heard how Lisa is doing? I tried to call the hospital yesterday, but they won't tell you anything unless you're family.

SUSAN. I have a friend who works there. She said Lisa's got a couple of broken bones, but she'll be fine.

JUDY. Broken bones! Oh my god! Poor Lisa!

SUSAN. And there's no head trauma, which is fortunate. He could have killed her outright. They've filled out a report.

CLARA. At least she's safe from him there. We should send her some flowers.

SUSAN. Once he's gone, we can. But we don't want to

antagonize him if anything goes wrong.

GARETH. I still can't believe he decided to go on a ski trip.

CLARA. What's he got to worry about? He told the paramedics she fell down the stairs.

GARETH. What kind of husband goes off to have fun while his wife is hospitalized?

SUSAN. She hasn't told the hospital what really happened. But they know. We've all been there.

(Everyone nods and murmurs agreement.)

Which makes it the perfect time. No one can pin it on LISA.

JUDY. I know.

SUSAN. And with him going, we have God to thank for providence.

GARETH. Amen to that. Judy, I can stop by after if you like.

JUDY. Maybe. I'm doing better now. Really.

GARETH. It's all figured out.

JUDY. I know.

CLARA. When are you going?

JUDY. Tomorrow. He's got a pass and he's staying at the lodge. I overheard him in the diner this morning bragging about how good he is. And you know what else? He actually flirted with me as he left. *(imitating)* "Oh. Hey hot mama." I. hate. him.

CLARA. That'll make it easier.

GARETH. Go get him, Tiger.

SUSAN. We'll look forward to hearing about it on the news.

JUDY. Do you think it'll be on the news?!

CLARA. And the papers.

GARETH. Something like this always makes the news.

CLARA. We'll all be saying prayers for you.

GARETH. And I'll bring the wine and chocolates after. You can vent to me about it all you like. Just text me when you head home.

JUDY. Can you make it whiskey?

GARETH. You betcha.

SUSAN. And I'll order the flowers.

Lights down.

SCENE 8 – THE NEXT DAY

Lights up. Susan and Clara are seated around a quilt frame, hand quilting a quilt throughout. The news plays on a radio or smartphone.

NEWSCASTER *(V.O.)* A skier was killed today while skiing in an out of bounds area of Stevens Pass.

(Clara gestures to Susan and they stop and listen.)

The man who died tumbled approximately 1,500 feet down a chute in the Tunnel Creek Canyon area. His fall triggered an avalanche. Initial reports of the avalanche reached the sheriff's office just after noon, and for some time it wasn't clear whether other skiers had also been swept up in the slide.

(Sound of the Newscaster dims but continues over Susan, Clara, and Gareth, below.)

The temperature at the top of the mountain was 22 degrees, according to the resort's website. The ski area's general manager said Sunday that the resort had received 22 inches of snow in the past 24 hours. He described the area as a popular backcountry skiing zone that can be easily accessed from the resort. He said the slopes there are steeper than at the resort and lack the resort's avalanche control. "You need to be a highly skilled skier to do that," he said. Recovery of the body was hampered as the avalanche is still very unstable. This marks the fourth fatality this year in the Cascades. The forecast is for another 15-20" of snow tonight. Ski lodges in the area are all selling out early due to heavy snow. It looks like we may have a record-breaking start to snowfall this winter.

CLARA. She did it. She did it.

SUSAN. She's safe.

CLARA. An avalanche. That's perfect.

SUSAN. An act of God.

(Enter Gareth.)

GARETH. I got a text message from Judy. It came in on my way here. *(reads out loud)* At Sheriff's office for questioning. Pray for me.

CLARA. Oh my God!

SUSAN. It could be nothing.

GARETH. What if someone saw her with him? What if she pushed him and someone saw?

SUSAN. Let's not start making up theories. We don't know anything yet.

GARETH. That's true. I was questioned. It was nothing, just when did you last see her, was she with anyone. Things like that. But what if they suspect. I'll bet they suspect.

SUSAN. Maybe she rode the ski lift up with him like she planned. Of course the police would want to interview her. I'm sure she's fine.

CLARA. Or they're going to charge her. Reckless homicide. Manslaughter. Who knows?

SUSAN. Stop that. We don't know what we don't know.

GARETH. You're right. She's just going in for an interview. He's back.

(Sound up and they stop and listen.)

NEWSCASTER. The identity of the body is being withheld pending notification of the family. Reports from witnesses state that the man had been drinking prior to riding the ski lift to the summit, and had argued with others about the conditions, after having been warned of avalanche risk. More after this commercial break.

(Sound dims to unintelligible commercial like sound)

CLARA. She better not say anything. About us, I mean.

SUSAN. She won't say anything.

GARETH. She's smart, Clara. I bet they'll be lucky to get more than one-word answers out of her.

CLARA. Judy?! You have met her, right?

SUSAN. She'll be fine. She knows what's at stake here. And she's doing a great job. It's just intimidating.

CLARA. I still have nightmares. The county Sheriff knocking on my door and snow's coming down and the power's out, and I'm standing there in my flannel pajamas and robe, and all I can think is, they're here to take me in.

SUSAN. This was before cellphones.

(Gareth nods.)

CLARA. So there I am, and he's asking me "Are you Mrs. Jenkins" and I'm nodding because I can't even speak, and I'm picturing being hauled away in my pajamas in handcuffs, and who's going to feed the cat? Because I just found out not even an hour earlier that my devil incarnate husband had just wrapped his car around a tree. And then I start shaking all over and -

SUSAN. - Remember what the Sheriff said?

CLARA. *(nodding)* I'm sorry but we need you to identify the body. *(beat)* That's it.

SUSAN. It's nothing. You'll see. What could possibly go wrong?

GARETH. Don't even say that out loud.

(Sound up.)

NEWSCASTER.   *(V.O.)* In other news, Seattle's annual Polar Bear plunge will take place this Saturday in Lake Union. It's expected to draw a large crowd this year in response to the challenge from New York City's Polar Bear plunge which drew over 300 people.

(The Newscaster V.O. fades as Lights go down.)

SCENE 9 – CHRISTMAS TIME

A Christmas tree is standing in one corner, with twinkly lights and quilted/sewing themed ornaments, rick rack garland, and presents underneath. Christmas music is playing. Judy and Lisa enter. They are in ugly Christmas sweaters and bundled up. Lisa is on crutches, with a boot or brace or cast, and Judy is hovering. Baby it's cold outside! In a perfect world, we could see snow falling out a window.

JUDY. Where is everybody? Here. Give me those things. I'll hang them up for you.

LISA. I can do it. God, you're worse than my mom.

JUDY. And then I'll find something to prop your foot up on, and I'll get you a lap quilt so you'll stay warm. Sit here. This chair's more comfortable.

LISA. Would you chill out?

JUDY. You were in traction for weeks. I just want to make sure you get all the way better.

(Judy grabs a box and a quilt from the shelves and brings them to Lisa.)

LISA. I know.

JUDY. Sit.

LISA. Fine. Happy?

(Judy props Lisa's foot on the box and drapes the quilt over Lisa's lap.)

JUDY. There. Now I'm happy. Comfortable?

LISA. Yes, thank you. Really.

JUDY. *(calling out)* Where are you guys? *(to Lisa)* They're here somewhere. Their stuff is under the table.

(Enter Susan, Clara, and Gareth with a cake or cupcakes.)

ALL. Welcome back!

GARETH. Just a little something to celebrate you getting out of the hospital.

(Susan and Gareth hand out punch.)

CLARA. I hope your mother didn't mind too much that we brought you here.

SUSAN. It's just a little something to welcome you home. To us.

LISA. She's still trying to process all of this. So am I. I guess I should be thanking you but I'm not sure this is... It still doesn't seem real. *(beat)* Is this gingerbread?

SUSAN. Your favorite. With cream cheese frosting.

LISA. You're so sweet!

GARETH. And it's about 5,000 calories a slice. But so worth it.

SUSAN. We just want you to know that you deserve all the happiness in the world.

(Susan raises a glass. Everyone responds.)

CLARA. Everything you've been denied.

GARETH. And we hope you have a long and happy life.

(Lisa is tearing up and she stops, suddenly sad. She puts down her cup.)

JUDY. No. No! You deserve happiness.

LISA. Not at the expense of someone else's life.

GARETH. You didn't deserve what he did to you.

LISA. I know.

CLARA. And besides, you haven't heard what happened.

SUSAN. It's not what you think at all.

LISA. Mark died. It's exactly what I think.

JUDY. No. You listen. I did go up there intending to push that jerk, sorry, Mark off the mountain. I really did. And everything went perfectly, just like we all discussed. But you need to know some things.

LISA. I feel so guilty! It was so hard to keep quiet at the hospital. I felt like everyone knew. Like they were all looking at me funny and just waiting for me to say the wrong thing and I'd be thrown in prison.

SUSAN. Nobody thought that. Honey, everyone at the hospital knew why you were there. They filed a domestic violence report right soon after you got there.

LISA. Mark told them I fell down the stairs.

SUSAN. You talk a lot when you're coming out of anesthesia.

LISA. *(to herself)* They were so nice to me... *(to everyone)* That's why they were so nice to me. It's all my fault. I shouldn't have said anything!

GARETH. You didn't do anything! You got beaten by a madman and barely survived. And Judy was ready and willing to give him a shove and wave to him as he went over the edge, but that's not the way it went.

LISA. It's not?

JUDY. I did go to the ski resort.

LISA. I know. Susan told me.

JUDY. But what you don't know is that he invited me to go with him.

LISA. What?

JUDY. He paid my lift ticket Then he took me to the Lodge for a drink. Well, he drank. Then he did a few lines –

(Judy continues over comment.)

CLARA. - Lines?

(Gareth imitates snorting cocaine, mouths cocaine.)

JUDY. - and so I stepped out to use the restroom and told the waitress to make all my drinks virgins. And she did. And you know what else? She said I was the third date he'd brought to the ski lodge in the last two weeks. I think she was trying to warn me.

GARETH. He'd been cheating on you while you were in the ICU.

LISA. That can't be right.

GARETH. Big time, sweetie.

JUDY. So anyway, he's downing drinks like the bar's about to close and he's as high as a kite and I'm getting pretty nervous by this time because, I mean, he's really drinking a lot.

GARETH. He'd had four drinks in a half hour.

JUDY. So then he wants to go skiing, and he's bragging about what a great skier he is, and how he's going to teach me some new moves on the slopes, and we head over to the ski lift. It's all going according to plan.

GARETH. But he's seriously drinking.

LISA. He drank sometimes at home, but never like that.

JUDY. Yeah, I remembered you said that, so I'm wondering what's the deal, but we head over to the ski lift, and he's feeling the effects of the alcohol, and so now he's starting to give other skiers a hard time. We rode up the first leg OK, but then he shoves this one guy and tells him to move over because he better let him go ahead of him in line. And people are starting to talk about him as he's dragging me past everyone. He's got my arm in a vise grip and we finally get to the front, and we get on the lift. By now I'm just glad he's sitting down because he's really acting weird, and I asked him, are you all right? And he asks me do I want a bump but I said no thanks.

(Gareth mimes snorting coke again. Clara nods.)

So now I'm really nervous because it takes time to get to the top, and it's a double black diamond trail coming down, and then - he starts talking about you.

LISA. Me?

JUDY. Yeah. And how he's got this life insurance policy, and when you die he's going to be rich.

LISA. Oh my God.

CLARA. His first attempt failed.

LISA. Oh my God! You think he was trying to murder me? *(beat)* How could I have been so stupid?

GARETH. Wait until you hear the rest.

JUDY. He bragged about how he was planning to start a charter boat business with the money. So there I am on the ski lift, trapped, and listening to Mark plot murder attempt number two. And let me tell you, I was not nervous anymore. I was seething.

LISA. We plotted to murder him too.

JUDY. I know! But at least we were trying to make you safe from him and his fists. He wanted to kill you so he could buy. a. boat.

(Lisa takes this in. She is no longer crying. Her demeanor changes.)

LISA. Tell me the rest.

JUDY. There's not a lot left to tell. So here he is celebrating his big plan. He's figured that when you got home from the hospital, he'd just slip you too many painkillers and then "hello boat". We finally got to the top and when we got off, Mark was so drunk and so high he could barely stay upright, and he went left instead of right, and off the trail towards the cliff. And then over. I just stood at the top and watched. *(beat)* I never laid a finger on him.

GARETH. We heard a news report that a skier had died, and we figured Judy had done the deed.

CLARA. But then Judy texted that she was at the police station, and we were all freaking out.

JUDY. *You* were freaking out? *I* was freaking out. I'm thinking they know something and I'm going to prison… but they just wanted a statement about my ride up the ski lift. The lodge had already told them about the drinks, and I told them about the coke. So...

SUSAN. You're safe. And everyone here is fine.

(Silence.)

LISA. I'm glad he's dead. He was a monster.

CLARA. That's the first time you've called him that. Good for you.

LISA. Why did I stay so long? All those years. All those beatings. I didn't deserve it. I didn't deserve any of it.

GARETH. He can't hurt you anymore. Ever.

LISA. You all saved me. Thank you.

CLARA. We've all been there.

JUDY. Every one of us. The police sure don't stop them.

CLARA. Or the courts. A restraining order isn't worth the paper it's written on.

GARETH. But we stop them. Now you'll never have to worry about him getting out on parole and coming after you.

JUDY. Or having to move away and change your name and hope they aren't smart enough to figure out where you went -

CLARA. Or live in constant fear, looking around every corner.

GARETH. We're all good people, Lisa. We're just problem solvers.

CLARA. And good friends. It's what good friends do.

SUSAN. If we couldn't rely on each other none of us would be here. And now you are a full member of our group. With all our secrets, and our support. And next time, someone will need your help.

(Lisa nods.)

CLARA. *(raising a glass)* To Charlene, and to our newest member, Lisa.

JUDY. Junior member.

SUSAN. Really? Judy...

JUDY. Well it's true.

(Gareth and Clara each get a present under the tree. A Christmas carol plays.)

GARETH. This one's for... Judy! Merry Christmas.

(Gareth crosses to Judy and hands her the gift.)

CLARA. Susan! I hope you like it.

(Clara hands a gift to SUSAN.)

SUSAN. You know I like getting anything.

(Susan opens her gift as Lisa watches. Gareth takes Judy aside.)

GARETH. Are you ever going to tell her the truth?

JUDY. One day maybe.

(They hand out gifts as lights go down.)

SCENE 10 – A FEW WEEKS LATER

Enter Lisa, fully recovered, carrying a large box of clothes. Judy and Clara are rolling out batting to cut out for a quilt top and back on the table. Susan is sewing at the machine, and Gareth enters from the back room.

LISA. Hey everyone!

GARETH. Here. Let me help you with that.

LISA. There's more in the trunk. Watch out for the icy sidewalk.

GARETH. I'll get them.

(Lisa hands the box to Gareth who takes it downstage and sets it down, then exits to retrieve more boxes.)

LISA. *(to Judy and Clara)* What are you doing?

CLARA. We're cutting a piece of batting for the quilt Judy's made.

LISA. For the middle.

JUDY. Yeah. It's the padding. I wanted super thick and fluffy, but Clara says it's easier to start with batting this thickness.

CLARA. She's going to try quilting it together on her machine at home.

(Gareth enters with a box.)

SUSAN. You're braver than me, Judy. I just turn them in and let Clara do her magic.

CLARA. Flatterer.

GARETH. Don't listen to her. Clara's machine quilting is

amazing.

LISA. Is it hard to do?

CLARA. In the beginning, but once you know all the tricks, it's not too bad.

JUDY. With a $10,000 computerized quilting set up. I must be out of my mind.

CLARA. You'll be fine. Remember, it's just a baby quilt.

JUDY. Just a baby quilt. It's four by five feet.

CLARA. Babies are very forgiving. Just do something simple like I showed you and you'll be fine.

LISA. Thanks for lugging them in, Gareth. I haven't sorted through any of this stuff yet. My Mom packed up anything Mark's family didn't want. She just threw the rest in boxes.

JUDY. They wanted his clothes?

LISA. Yeah. When I was still in the hospital. They took his biker jacket, and his letterman jacket. Stuff like that.

CLARA. And you had no chance to say no? That's horrible.

LISA. Good riddance. He didn't own a motorcycle. He won the jacket from some contest at the Harley Davidson down in Seattle. It didn't even fit him. And he lettered in bench warming for football.

GARETH. I'd be happy to help you sort.

SUSAN. Gareth is really good with fabrics. Not everything works in a quilt.

GARETH. Now if this gets to be too much for you, just say the word and we'll stop.

LISA. OK.

(They open the boxes.)

GARETH. Just set aside anything made out of denim or

canvas, like jeans or heavy-duty coveralls, things like that.

SUSAN. We sell them to a wholesaler who sends the denim to be repurposed into money.

LISA. What?

SUSAN. Really. U.S. dollars are made from old denim. Look at it sometime. You can make out the little bits of thread and everything.

JUDY. And the rest goes to the recycler in China. China buys fabric in bulk. By the pound.

GARETH. It's one way we get money for batting and such.

LISA. I don't think there's a lot left. He wore jeans and coveralls most of the time. Oh. Here's a shirt I gave him for Christmas that he never wore.

GARETH. Plaids. These'll work.

CLARA. The flannel ones pieced together make some nice cozy backings.

LISA. His wedding suit.

(Everyone stops to see her reaction.)

Susan, can I borrow your scissors, please?

(Susan hands her the scissors. Lisa starts chopping apart the suit, escalating to ripping as she goes.)

This is for making me buy you this stupid suit. And this is for promising me a honeymoon in Hawaii and then cancelling so you could go to the boat races. And this is for that time you knocked me out in the kitchen! And this is for every time you used me as your personal punching bag! And this is for trying to kill me, you asshole.

GARETH. Hey, hey! Steady there.

LISA. Oh. Wow, I don't know what came over me.

GARETH. Alright then. Let's just put the scissors down and take a minute shall we?

(Gareth takes the scissors and hands them back to Susan.)

LISA. I'm fine. I'm great! I never felt so alive in my life. I've been having nightmares about you coming back and getting me, but this...this is the most powerful feeling. I'm free. You can't hurt me anymore, you Monster.

GARETH. Just take a breath.

(Lisa breathes.)

Better?

JUDY. That was awesome!

LISA. *(embarrassed)* I'm sorry. I must seem like a nutcase right now.

CLARA. No. No! We've all reacted in our own way. Yours is just... unique. Feel better?

JUDY. I knew you were one of us. Channeling your inner bitch!

(Judy high-fives Lisa.)

LISA. I am. I don't have to hold back or worry about what anybody thinks of me. You're all here for me. Thank you.

GARETH. It's very cathartic.

LISA. Like a huge knot just untied in my stomach.

SUSAN. I think you're in the anger phase. We've all been there at some point.

(Lisa resumes sorting. She tosses out items into a pile)

LISA. This is good for a quilt, right?

GARETH. Yeah.

LISA. And how about this? And this?

GARETH. Mm-hmm.

LISA. Here's a couple more. The rest of this box is just socks and underwear. Why did my mother pack those?

GARETH. We can go through the rest of these later, but they're mostly jeans.

LISA. OK. And you know what I'm going to do this afternoon?

GARETH. What's that, hon?

LISA. I'm going to look for a job.

Lights down.

SCENE 11 – TWO YEARS LATER. FALL

Lights up on Susan, Clara, and Gareth busy setting up. Susan tries to lift a bin.

SUSAN. Gareth would you be a dear and help me with this? I can usually manage but...

CLARA. I'll get it. You need to stop trying to do the heavy stuff, SUSAN.

GARETH. Are you still having trouble?

SUSAN. After all these years, you'd think I'd be better. I'm going to go take something for the pain.

(Susan exits. Clara gets a quilt, sits, and begins sewing the binding)

CLARA. It's amazing she survived. That scum took so much from her.

GARETH. That's why she never could have children, isn't it? She'd have been a terrific mother.

CLARA. Remember that little girl at the parade?

GARETH. The goat.

CLARA. She finds ways to mother kids.

(Judy enters.)

ALL. Sorry sorry!

JUDY. I know. I was supposed to be here a half hour ago but -

GARETH. - You lost track of the time. It's OK. You're here now. Here. Give me your coat.

SUSAN. *(O.S.)* Where's the Tylenol?

CLARA. It's above the sink.

SUSAN. *(O.S.)*. Got it!

JUDY. I brought pumpkin pie for later.

SUSAN. *(O.S)* God bless Judy!

CLARA. How are you doing today, Gareth? It's the anniversary, isn't it?

GARETH. Yeah. I thought about not coming earlier this week, but when I woke up this morning, I hadn't had any nightmares and I didn't even remember what day it was until I looked at my calendar after breakfast.

JUDY. I'm sorry! We should have done this another day, GARETH.

GARETH. I'm doing fine. Really. I think I'm finally moving on. How about you Clara?

CLARA. I'd do it again in a heartbeat. She was a monster.

JUDY. Wow, Clara. Tell us how you really feel!

CLARA. Sorry. Sorry, Gareth.

(Clara hugs Gareth.

GARETH. Hey. You saved me, Clara. It's OK. Really.

(Susan enters with a glass of water. Enter Lisa carrying a takeout bag of BBQ.)

JUDY. Hey, Lisa! You made it! I didn't expect you to come. I thought you had to work.

LISA. I got done early. Here's the order you asked for, SUSAN.

(Lisa hands her the bag)

JUDY. I'll get another chair. So how is the job going? I haven't seen you in a while.

(Judy exits and returns with a folding chair. She sets it up.)

GARETH. Our very own on-air reporter. We're all so proud of you.

LISA. I just landed a feature assignment I've been pitching forever.

SUSAN. You look so happy.

LISA. It's a big deal. With luck you'll see me doing an interview next week on the evening news.

JUDY. Wow! Congratulations.

LISA. No more bits on parades and fluff pieces. I'm interviewing the Head of the Seattle Women's Shelter. Finally. It only took two years.

GARETH. Someday we'll be able to say we knew her when.

CLARA. This smells really good.

SUSAN. Lunch. My treat. Actually it's the reason I called you all in today.

CLARA. Another potential member for the group.

SUSAN. You're way ahead of me.

CLARA. How bad is it?

SUSAN. Bad enough.

LISA. How did you -

GARETH. It takes one to know one.

JUDY. So. Let's hear it. Who is she?

GARETH. Or he.

JUDY. Statistically you're an outlier.

GARETH. But not impossible. So, Susan?

SUSAN. She's young. Younger than most.

JUDY. Called it!

CLARA. It's the young girl at the Barbeque place. The one that won't make eye contact.

SUSAN. You were right, as usual, Clara. When you first told me about her, I wasn't sure. I mean, the way she presents is like general anxiety, or maybe even just super shy.

CLARA. *(to Lisa)* See? Postal workers. We're invisible.

(Lisa giggles.)

SUSAN. I checked with my friends at the hospital. It's getting tougher now. My friends there have moved on, so I had to dip into our funds.

JUDY. You hired a detective?

SUSAN. No. I just had to resort to a little bribe to an admin.

GARETH. I hope you gave them cash! Anything else could be traceable.

SUSAN. No. I just bought tickets to the Broadway tour of a show I know he loves.

GARETH. You're kidding me.

CLARA. Genius.

LISA. But how -

SUSAN. I stopped by and told him I had these tickets I couldn't use, and I thought of him. Then we started chatting about my neighbor and how I wanted to make her something special since she's been down lately, but I was worried because I knew she might have allergies and...

CLARA. And you got him to look up her medical record.

SUSAN smiles.

CLARA. And it confirmed my suspicions.

(Susan nods.)

GARETH. Susan, you never cease to amaze me. That took guts.

SUSAN. I just knew a guy who could help. The credit should really go to Clara. She spotted her.

CLARA. She looks so scared. She can't be more than about 25. I've bought a lot of Barbeque lately so we could chat. Her name is Ashley.

SUSAN. Lisa, what did you think? You picked up the Barbeque.

LISA. She did seem kind of nervous. She's so tiny. Is that big guy in the back with all the tattoos her husband?

CLARA. Yes.

SUSAN. Two spiral fractures of her arms in the last year alone.

LISA. That's terrifying.

CLARA. I know! I googled him. And he's got a profile on Tinder.

JUDY. What a sleaze.

SUSAN. So, what does everyone think? Shall we take a vote to invite her in?

(All raise their hand in turn, until Lisa. She finally joins in.)

JUDY. Now it's your turn.

LISA. I know. *(to Judy)* Like you did for me.

JUDY. I didn't do anything. He just fell –

(Lisa shakes her head and smiles.)

LISA. I know what you did. I've always known.

(Hugging JUDY.)

You gave me back my life.

JUDY. Just paying it forward, LISA.

SUSAN. Let's give Ashley back hers.

LISA. You're right. Let's do this. I mean, how hard can it be?

SUSAN. When you plan it right, it doesn't take much at all. Sometimes you don't even have to be there when they go.

CLARA. You just move a ladder.

GARETH. Or take the life vests out of the boat. And make a little hole.

SUSAN. Or mess with the brake fluid on a car.

JUDY. Or give them a little shove when they aren't looking.

LISA. *(laughing)* You make it sound so easy.

GARETH. It's not as hard as you think.

CLARA. And afterwards we can make a lovely quilt!

(All rise. Clara unfolds a beautiful quilt.)

GARETH. Oh Clara, you've outdone yourself.

SUSAN. I love the pattern. It's so...alive.

LISA. Is that Mark's shirt?

CLARA. Mm-hum. And these two colors should be familiar too.

LISA. I still can't believe old clothes can make such amazing quilts.

CLARA. In the end, it's just paying it forward. Now, all this needs is a label.

GARETH. What are you going to call it?

CLARA. I don't know. Lisa? What do you think?

LISA. Hm. How about "Nothing Wasted"?

SUSAN. That's perfect.

JUDY. To paying it forward.

LISA. Nothing gets wasted.

ALL. Except them!

(All raise up the quilt in unity, smiling, celebrating. They are a team. Lights down.)

END OF PLAY

71

Acknowledgements

I've always been a huge fan of dark comedies. "Arsenic and Old Lace", and "Fargo" are two great examples of this genre. It's reality but heightened. Extreme. I knew when I came up with the idea for Crazy Quilts that it was going to be a dark but funny ride. I first wrote Crazy Quilts in 2019. It was a ten-minute play with fast twists and a fun gotcha moment. It went on to win many awards and productions and was published in "The Best Short Plays of 2021" (Smith & Kraus). What I didn't expect was everyone asking, "But then what happened?", and I knew I needed to do a much deeper dive into a sensitive, and often unspoken topic. That's how the full-length version of Crazy Quilts came about.

This play is about the real struggles of mostly women, traumatized, both emotionally and physically, where there is no one to turn to, no safety, and no escape, and those who have been there, stepping up and coming to their aid when society fails them. A lot of my research went into what happens to the traumatized, what kind of tactics are used against them, how they are worn down by their oppressors, and how they try to maintain a veneer of normalcy, all while often in near total denial of their situation.

Many scenes contain direct quotes from real people. Quilting is a huge hobby in the Pacific Northwest, and I am thankful to all my fellow quilters for their support in coming to see the play as it developed and offering insights and reactions throughout the process. Quilters are a close-knit group, support each other both artistically and personally, and make art out of cast offs, scraps, and unfinished objects. They are meticulous, with amazing attention to detail, and incredibly creative. What better support group could there be?

I'm thankful to all the theaters that helped in the development of Crazy Quilts. It takes place on a small fictitious island in the Puget Sound off the coast of Washington, and most of the readings were done in theaters in that area. When Crazy Quilts was being workshopped, I was amazed to have people who have lived through experiences like this who came to me and said how it rang true, and how important it was to help people better understand it. They said the comedy made the truths within it relatable without being so dark that it would be tough to sit through. They thanked me for writing it. Some found it triggering, yet cathartic. Some cried. They all said they laughed.

And last, and most importantly, thank you to Owen Robertson and LAB Theatre Project for the confidence and hard work from everyone, a great cast and crew, all bringing Crazy Quilts to the stage. This was Crazy Quilts premiere, and I am in awe of their work ethic and attention to detail. They went through two hurricanes and resumed rehearsals the following Monday. Now that's dedication. I hope that when you experience Crazy Quilts you will laugh, feel the struggles of each character, and discuss it on your way home.

- Karen Fix Curry

NOTES

(Use this space to make notes for your production)

GATHER BY THE GHOST LIGHT is a storytelling podcast in radio theater format. Think of the Ghost Light as your campfire. Gather around and listen to stories from a variety of genres. Playwright Jonathan Cook and Devon McSherry are the hosts of the series and most of the stories you hear were originally written as short stage plays and they now have been adapted to audio plays with professional voice actors and immersive sound effects. The audio plays produced on this podcast give these talented playwrights an even wider audience for their stories. We welcome you to join us in this journey as we extend the voices of emerging playwrights!

Available wherever you get your podcasts!
For more information, please visit:
www.gatherbytheghostlight.com

Gather by the Ghost Light annual anthologies of audio plays produced on the podcast are all available through Ghost Light Publications!

BOBBY IS DEAD
by Marty Matfess

Chris has been madly in love with his best friend Annie for years, but she's only been interested in dating everyone else but him. After Annie's recent break up with her boyfriend Bobby, Chris feels this may finally be what he needs to find his way into her heart, but just like that ... she's already moved on to another guy she met at a coffee shop. Being the good friend that he is, Chris has agreed to hang out with the new guy's visiting sister while they go out on a date. Oh, and let's not forget about Bobby. Turns out he's not taking the break up too well and Chris is now caught between an aggressive ex-boyfriend while having to keep new guy's sister company. A play about love, lust, and getting shot in the head.

IN THE SLUSH
by Daniel Prillaman

2023 FINALIST FOR NEW DRAMATISTS' PRINCESS GRACE AWARD

Newlywed Laura Beth Gardner has it all. A loving husband, a baby on the way, and a usually delightful job. But this weekend, tasked with reading through her publishing house's slush pile, she encounters a mysterious manuscript that claims she isn't human. That her husband isn't who he says he is. And that she's a vessel for her unborn child, who is actually the Second Coming of an ancient darkness that will devour the world. It has to be some sort of joke.

…But what if it's not?

A cosmic horror about identity, creation, and the things we'll do to realize our dreams.

KINGDUMB
by Jonathan Cook

There's a new King in the land that has initiated a mysterious new tax on the citizens. Outraged, the region's finest Clock fixer, aka "Time Repair Specialist", recruits some of the most unlikely rebels to help him develop a plan to overthrow the King. Their plotting takes them on a comedic journey through perilous mountain tops all the way to the palace itself where they confront this vile King face to face. Kingdumb is a medieval fantasy comedy full of absurdist humor and illogical behavior.

ALL BARK, NO BITE
by Kara Emily Krantz

Charlotte and Eugene live a quiet, no-nonsense lifestyle surrounded by sudoku and argyle. Robert and Bella are boisterous and messy and ridiculously in love. Then there's the neighbor, Suzanne, who basically doesn't know what's going on, but definitely has something to say about it. Sure, relationships can be exciting! They can also be confusing, unexpected, and expose us to profound emotional risk. However, relationships are almost always worth exploring, and if we're willing to be vulnerable, can fill up the empty or wounded spaces in our hearts. And if that doesn't work? Well, get a dog.

THE ROCK AND THE HARD PLACE

by Emily McClain

Alan Tully was convicted of the murder of Janice Beck in 1996 and has been on death row for 23 years, during which time he has maintained his innocence. His daughter Elsie receives a letter from the man who claims to have committed the crime and she attempts to use the information to exonerate her father. The insurmountable challenges of exonerating a wrongly convicted person drive her to the desperate position of threatening a man she believes could help free her father, with disastrous results.

BREAKING THE SHAKESPEARE CODE

by John Minigan

Anna arrives in a college rehearsal hall, hoping to get advice from intimidating acting instructor Curt about landing the lead in a professional production of Romeo and Juliet. Once he agrees to help, they embark on sixteen years of emotional entanglements that reshape both of their lives.

www.ghostlightpubs.com